Sammy & Sue Go Green Too!

Suzanne Corso

BEAUFORT
BOOKS

To get more information and to order Sammy & Sue books
please visit our web site

www.SammyandSue.com

ISBN: 978-0-8253-0517-7

Library of Congress Cataloging-in-Publication data available

Published in the United States by Beaufort Books, New York
www.beaufortbooks.com

Distributed by Midpoint Trade Books, New York
www.midpointtrade.com

Printed in China

This book is dedicated to our
motherlove, planet earth;

A place for our children to flourish!

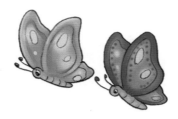

Sammy and Sue set out
on green adventures

Unaware they would run into
surprising temperatures.

Pollution and global warming,
could leave the earth destroyed.

They soon discovered there was more they could do
than sit back and be annoyed.

As Sammy and Sue geared up
they knew what they had to do.

They sat down to watch a climate conscious show
on a nature channel, too.

It had a message they just couldn't ignore.
Sammy said: "We have to save our environment;
that is our number one chore!"

So off they went with backpacks
and filtered water bottles in hand.

Sammy and Sue had one mission in mind
and that was to save the land.

Off to the organic farmers and eco-friendly companies,
their first journey had begun.

It wouldn't be easy, but their passion and drive
would turn their hard work into fun.

Sammy was happy to see that organic farmers
grow their crops so free.

"Their food is made without any pesticides
or hormones to harm little me."

"Think of all the good we could do!"
Mommy Sue shouted out.

"I just know that the children will listen,
I haven't any doubt."

So Sammy and Sue
continued with their adventure,
uncovering the next eco-treasure.

Finding all sorts of great green products
to try out and use with pleasure.

Ingredients like baking soda,
lemons, and lavender oil will keep us clean,

By creating a safe haven for kids
so they can be green.

They found that their first company provides
healthy, natural products for kids with heart.

While another company makes it easy for grown-ups
to have a clean kitchen, right from the start.

They found non-toxic, natural cleaning choices
that are safe and smart,

Using these pure cleaners really works,
if you are willing to start.

To their amazement
they found natural cottons
and green laundry soap,

Organic toothpaste, mouthwash,
and biodegradable shampoo,
which gave them hope.

Sammy and Sue stopped by a local,
organic health-food store.

To sample their candies, ice cream,
herbal teas, and so much more!

They soon realized how much healthier
these organic foods are for you.

No impurities, no sugars, just more energy
for the things you love to do!

"It really was quite simple to see...
That being able to save the environment
was right in front of me!"

Sammy exclaimed, with joy in her heart:
"I can even wear a carbon-free tee-shirt
displaying my own art."

On their latest trip Sammy and Sue
raised environmental awareness,
By letting people know about recyclable products
and consumer fairness.

Sammy and Sue now love to drive hybrid cars,
Because they don't pollute the atmosphere,
while they gaze at the movie stars.

Actors and singers and our favorite performers
are in on this green quest,
To save the earth from all of the harmful impurities,
we ALL must try our best.

Mommy Sue says: "So with all we know,
we ask you to conserve, preserve, reserve, and spare.

And always, always, always be aware

This is our planet, our own heaven on earth,
for which we must care.

Let's keep it alive and beautiful
so we can nourish our days.

We'll keep our world safe and free
by adapting eco-friendly ways."

The End

Five Fun Facts

1. Our green environment can only stay pure if we all help, that means purchasing from eco-friendly companies.

2. Driving a hybrid car can produce 90% less pollutants than a non-hybrid car, and adds less harmful chemicals to the atmosphere.

3. Eating organic can not only help the environment, but make our bodies healthier.

4. Our parks are natural places, so let's preserve them by not littering. Always recycle.

5. We must do our part as little people to conserve energy. That means shutting off lights and turning off running faucets.

Hard Words Made Easy

(Also known as the Glossary)

Atmosphere — the air surrounding Earth.

Biodegradable — capable of breaking down over time, usually designed to do so quickly, completely, and safely.

Carbon-free — something that does not produce Carbon Dioxide, which is harmful to our atmosphere.

Climate conscious — making decisions that help the environment, not ones that hurt it.

Consumer fairness — making sure that companies treat their customers right by being honest and fair in their practices.

Eco-friendly — using goods and services that cause the least harm possible to the environment.

Environment — all that surrounds us--the air, soil, oceans, etc.

Going Green — living a life that has the least impact on the environment which includes using organic products, conserving energy, and recycling.

Hormones — harmful substances in food that can be avoided by eating organic and free-range.

Hybrid car — a vehicle that uses more than one power source like gas and electricity, which helps cut down on pollution.

Non-toxic — non-toxic substances are safe and do not produce poisons.

Organic — grown without using harmful chemicals or pesticides.

Pesticides — harmful chemicals used to protect plants from insects.

Pollution — the introduction of harmful materials to water, land, and air.

Recycle — the process of using a substance over and over again, even for different purposes.

Eco-Friendly Endorsments

"Sammy & Sue are imaginative stories that will capture your child's attention, entertain them while educating them on the beautiful and delicate balance of our ecosystem. In time, these stories are destined to become classics much along the lines of Dr. Seuss with a meaningful message delivered through an engaging storyline."

—John Replogle, President & CEO, Burt's Bees

"Sammy & Sue are a wonderful way for young children to learn about the planet and be introduced to important environmental issues affecting our health and that of the world."

—Jack Murray, Director National Resources Defense Council

"Sammy & Sue bring a sense of adventure to some of the most important lessons of our time, making it fun for children and adults alike to raise their awareness of the challenges our planet faces."

—Celestial Seasonings

"In today's fast paced world of constant changing and global needs, we are happy to acknowledge that Sammy & Sue are making environmentally educational books that will surpass many."

—Method Products, Inc. People Against Dirty

"Endearing and informative, Sammy & Sue effortlessly bring valuable green lessons to life. We are pleased to support the commitment to educating children about organic farming and living."

—Horizon Organic

"To bring about positive environmental change requires an understanding of our impact on the natural world, and a sense of adventure with endless possibility; Sammy & Sue have both."

—Philip Charles Gamett, President EarthPositive Apparel

"Through their diverse and engaging explorations, Sammy & Sue demonstrate the invaluable role all families can play in conservation efforts around the world and in our own backyards."

—Jim Knox, Wildlife Educator, Television Host - Wild Zoofari

"Through a touching mother-daughter bond, Sammy & Sue convey common sense and environmental advice through loving and naturalistic conversation. The result is a pleasant and educational journey for a parent and child to share together."

—Virginia Chipurnoi, President - Humane Society of New York

"We're proud to endorse this great book that promotes environmental stewardship and creates positive change across the planet."

— Ryan Black, CEO/founder, Sambazon, The ACAI Berry

"There aren't two more important issues today than the well being of our children and the quality of our world and the air we breath. Sammy & Sue have done a great job of protecting both our planet and our children. Hats off to such a noble effort."

— Steve Demos, Chairman and Co-Founder

"Your friends at Simple are proud to support Sammy & Sue, who open our children's minds to the importance of environmental stewardship, and living a healthy life based on conservation."

—Simple Shoes

"Kids, read Sammy & Sue....and be smart-aah, live healthi-aah, and know your planet bett-aah!"

—Rose Cameron, Founder, WAT-AAH!

PROUD SAMMY & SUE SUPPORTERS

Other Sammy & Sue Books

(coming soon)

SAMMY & SUE EATING ORGANIC AND EXERCISING TOO!!!
SAMMY & SUE WITH DOLPHINS AND OCEANS TOO!!!

SAMMY & SUE ON CONSERVING ENERGY TOO!!!
SAMMY & SUE WITH LIONS AND TIGERS TOO!!!

SAMMY & SUE WITH RECYCLABLE THINGS TOO!!!
SAMMY & SUE WITH BEACHES AND SHELLS TOO!!!

SAMMY & SUE DRIVING HYBRID CARS TOO!!!
SAMMY & SUE WITH ELEPHANTS IN AFRICA TOO!!!

SAMMY & SUE WITH GORILLAS AND RAINFORESTS TOO!!!
SAMMY & SUE WITH BEES AND HONEY TOO!!!

SAMMY & SUE WITH DUCKS AND PONDS AND FISH AND LAKES TOO!!!
SAMMY & SUE WITH MONKEYS AND TREES TOO!!!

SAMMY & SUE AND COOKING WITH FAMILY TOO!!!
SAMMY & SUE AND SIPPING TEA TOO!!!

SAMMY & SUE WITH DOGS AND PARKS TOO!!!
SAMMY & SUE WITH BEARS AND BOATS TOO!!!

Please visit the **Sammy & Sue** web site to

Learn more about the books, and,

Sammy & Sue's Green World

An eco-friendly online Virtual World for Kids

www.SammyandSue.com

Praise for Sammy & Sue

"Sammy & Sue and the Girl Scouts have a common commitment to making the world a better place. They discover and connect with each other and their world, and then take action to help the environment."

- Magali Vasquez, Director of Program,
Girl Scout Council of Greater New York

"Life's lessons dramatized with a tender regard for the innocence of children."

-Olympia Dukakis,
Academy Award Winning Actress

"By bringing awareness to protecting the environment, Suzanne Corso will teach your children well."

-Lorraine Bracco,
Academy Award Nominated Actress

"A hip testament to being kind to the world around us"

-Dr. Mehmet Oz, Columbia University,
Vice Chairman, Cardiovascular Services,
Oprah Show/XM Radio

"These wonderful stories instill a sense of not only understanding but, empowerment to our children about the earth and how to take care of it. I look forward to reading them with my daughters."

-Marcia Cross,
Actress "Desperate Housewives" ABC

"A winning collection of stories clearly makes these books perfect."

-David Cone,
Major league baseball player, Cy Young Award
Winner 94-Perfect Game-NY 1999

"Corso has created a mother-daughter relationship in her books that will be inspirational to all parents. Her educational as well as, wonderfully entertaining storylines will be a delight to read for children of all ages."

-Joyce Dewitt, Actress (Three's Company)

"Sammy & Sue" are a delightful mother-daughter team exploring fascinating ways to become more "Earth-friendly". Today's youngsters are tomorrow's Earth stewards, and this series of books is an inspiring resource!"

-Jack Hanna, Director Emeritus,
Columbus Zoo, TV's Wildlife Expert

"Here is an amazing book about a mother and daughter's electrifying journey into the world of science and nature. It enhances a child's awareness of her role in protecting the environment as she ventures into an illuminating discovery with her mother."

-Mrs. Concepcion R. Alvar,
Headmistress of Marymount School,
New York City

"A wonderfully crafted series of environmentally educational reading, with the added twist of inspiration that the world needs today."

-William T. Sullivan,
president & CEO,
Ronald McDonald House